jE THAL

The teac. S0-ATV-178

 Black Lagoon and other
stories.
Thaler, Mike,

NOV 07 2014

THE PRINCIPAL FROM THE
BLACK LAGOON

**STORY BY
MIKE THALER**

**PICTURES BY
JARED LEE**

**Cartwheel
B·O·O·K·S**®

SCHOLASTIC INC.

New York   Toronto   London   Auckland   Sydney
Mexico City   New Delhi   Hong Kong   Buenos Aires

For Bill Rich
and all principals
who love kids.
— M.T.

For Dad, who always encouraged
this kid to draw.
— J.L.

No part of this publication may be reproduced in whole or in part, stored in a retrieval system, or transmitted in any form or by any means, electronic, mechanical, photocopying, recording, or otherwise, without written permission of the publisher. For information regarding permission, write to Scholastic Inc., Attention: Permissions Department, 557 Broadway, New York, NY 10012.

ISBN-13: 978-545-06932-8
ISBN-10: 0-545-06932-7

Text copyright © 1993 by Mike Thaler.
Illustrations copyright © 1993 by Jared D. Lee Studio, Inc.

All rights reserved. Published by Scholastic Inc.
SCHOLASTIC, CARTWHEEL BOOKS, and associated logos
are trademarks and/or registered trademarks of Scholastic Inc.

Library of Congress Cataloging-in-Publication Data is available.

10 9   40   13 14 15/0
Printed in the U.S.A. · This edition first printing, September 2008

It's the third day of school.
I've been sent to the principal's office.
What a bummer!

I hear the principal, Mrs. Green, is a real monster.

Kids go to her office and never come back.

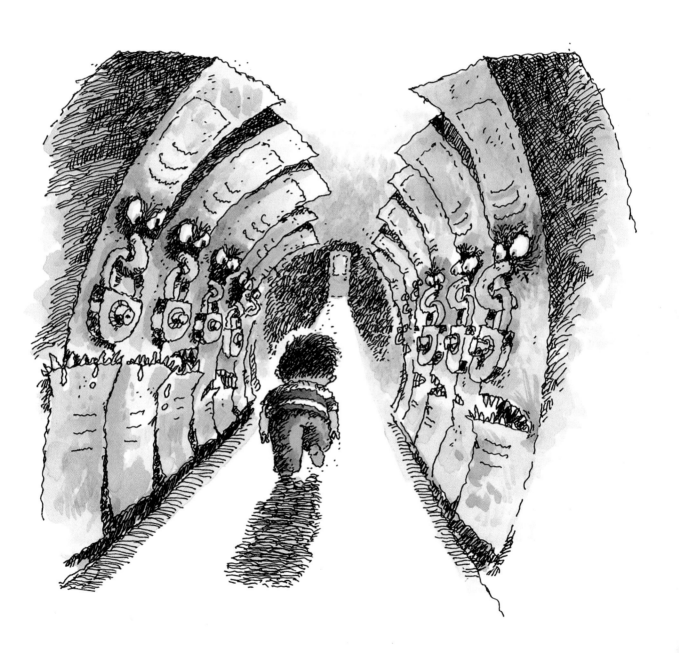

The waiting room is supposed to be filled with bones and skeletons.

Doris Foodle was sent there for chewing gum.

They say her skeleton still has a bubble in its mouth.

I walk in.
I take a seat.
The rug is red.
That's so the blood won't show.

PRINCIPAL

I hear she uses tall kids as coatracks.

The short kids she feeds to her pet alligator.

The fat ones she uses as paperweights.

The thin ones she uses as bookmarks.

I'm too young to be a bookmark!

Then there's her twelve-foot paddle.
It's supposed to have poisoned spikes on it.

If you're lucky you get put in "the cages."
She has them under the desk.

If you're *really* lucky you get sent home in chains.

But most kids she keeps for her *experiments*.

Derek Bloom was sent here yesterday.
They say he wound up with the head of a dog.

They say Freddy Jones has the feet of a chicken,

and Eric Porter, the hands of a hamster.

I'm too good-looking to have the ears of a rabbit!

All I did was snatch Mrs. Jones's wig.

It's very quiet today.

Usually, they say, there's a lot of screaming.

Maybe she's in a good mood.

Even if I survive, this will affect my whole life.

In the future I'll be running for president.
I'll be ahead in the polls.

And then it will come out!

I can see the headlines…

Oh-oh, there's a shadow at the glass.
Now I'm in the *jaws of fate*.

The door slowly opens.

There's a pretty woman standing there.
She's a master of disguise.

"Come in, Hubie."

I go in.

She closes the door behind me.

I look around.
There's only the coatrack.
It doesn't look like anyone I know.

I look around for the alligator.

There's only a turtle.

It looks a little like Randy Potts.

"Now," says Mrs. Green. "Are we having a little trouble in class?"
"Well," says I, "I was sweeping up the room and by accident
Mrs. Jones's wig got caught on the broom handle."

"Well, we'll have to apologize, won't we?"

"Yes, we will."

"And the next time, *we'll* have to be more careful."

"Yes, we will! Yes, we will!"

"Now run along."

"Is that *all*???"

"Close the door."

Boy, was I lucky.

Those flowers on her desk were probably poisonous.

Just one whiff and you would turn purple and die.

Fortunately I held my breath.

I went into her cave and I have returned without the ears of a rabbit.

I'll have to sweep *her* office sometime and see if *she* wears a wig!